USED BOOK

MAY 0 5 REC'D

Sold to Aztec Shops, Ltd.

*Ourika*

## Texts and Translations

Chair: English Showalter
Series editors: Jane K. Brown, Edward M. Gunn, Carol S. Maier,
Rachel May, Margaret Rosenthal, and Kathleen Ross

The Texts and Translations series was founded in 1991 to provide students and teachers with important texts not readily available or not available at an affordable price and in high-quality translations. The books in the series are intended for students in upper-level undergraduate and graduate courses in national literatures in languages other than English, comparative literature, ethnic studies, area studies, translation studies, women's studies, and gender studies. The Texts and Translations series is overseen by an editorial board composed of specialists in several national literatures and in translation studies.

### Texts

1. Isabelle de Charrière. *Lettres de Mistriss Henley publiées par son amie.* Ed. Joan Hinde Stewart and Philip Stewart. 1993.
2. Françoise de Graffigny. *Lettres d'une Péruvienne.* Introd. Joan DeJean and Nancy K. Miller. 1993.
3. Claire de Duras. *Ourika.* Ed. Joan DeJean. Introd. Joan DeJean and Margaret Waller. 1994.
4. Eleonore Thon. *Adelheit von Rastenberg.* Ed. and introd. Karin A. Wurst. 1996.
5. Emilia Pardo Bazán. *"El encaje roto" y otros cuentos.* Ed. and introd. Joyce Tolliver. 1996.
6. Marie Riccoboni. *Histoire d'Ernestine.* Ed. Joan Hinde Stewart and Philip Stewart. 1998.
7. Dovid Bergelson. *Opgang.* Ed. and introd. Joseph Sherman. 1999.

### Translations

1. Isabelle de Charrière. *Letters of Mistress Henley Published by Her Friend.* Trans. Philip Stewart and Jean Vaché. 1993.
2. Françoise de Graffigny. *Letters from a Peruvian Woman.* Trans. David Kornacker. 1993.
3. Claire de Duras. *Ourika.* Trans. John Fowles. 1994.
4. Eleonore Thon. *Adelheit von Rastenberg.* Trans. George F. Peters. 1996.
5. Emilia Pardo Bazán. *"Torn Lace" and Other Stories.* Trans. María Cristina Urruela. 1996.
6. Marie Riccoboni. *The Story of Ernestine.* Trans. Joan Hinde Stewart and Philip Stewart. 1998.
7. Dovid Bergelson. *Descent.* Trans. Joseph Sherman. 1999.

# CLAIRE DE DURAS

# *Ourika*
## *An English Translation*

Translated and with a Foreword by
John Fowles

Introduction by
Joan DeJean and Margaret Waller

The Modern Language Association of America
New York   1994

Translation and foreword ©1994 by J. R. Fowles Ltd.
Introduction by Joan DeJean and Margaret Waller
©1994 by The Modern Language Association of America.
All rights reserved. Printed in the United States of America

For information about obtaining permission to reprint material from
MLA book publications, send your request by mail (see address below),
e-mail (permissions@mla.org), or fax (646-458-0030).

Library of Congress Cataloging-in-Publication Data

Duras, Claire de Durfort, duchesse de, 1777–1828.
[Ourika. English]
Ourika : an English translation / Claire de Duras ; translated and
with a foreword by John Fowles ; introduction by Joan DeJean and
Margaret Waller.
p.   cm. — (Texts and translations. Translations ; 3)
Includes bibliographic references.
ISBN 0-87352-780-1 (paper)
1. France—Race relations—19th century—Fiction. 2. Women,
Black—France—Fiction. 3. Africans—France—Fiction. I. Fowles,
John, 1926–   . II. Title. III. Series.
PQ2235.D650813   1994
843' .7—dc20                          94-36092
ISSN 1079-2538

Cover illustration: *Portrait d'une négresse*, by Marie-Guillemine
Benoist (1768–1826). Reprinted by courtesy of La Réunion des
Musées Nationaux, Paris, France

Third printing. Set in Dante. Printed on recycled paper

Published by The Modern Language Association of America
26 Broadway, New York, New York 10004-1789
www.mla.org

# TABLE OF CONTENTS

# INTRODUCTION

Claire-Louise Lechat de Coëtnempren de Kersaint (1777–1828) was born into the generation and the class destined to feel most intensely and most protractedly the trauma generated by the French Revolution. Her father, the count of Kersaint, was a member of the liberal aristocracy that supported the Revolution during its early years. He refused to vote in favor of Louis XVI's execution, however, and shared his king's fate. After his death, Claire and her mother fled France, stopping briefly in Philadelphia en route to her mother's native Martinique to recover Mme de Kersaint's considerable inheritance. Their exile later continued in Switzerland and finally in London, with its important émigré community. There Claire met her husband, Amédée-Bretagne-Malo de Durfort, duke of Durfort and future duke of Duras, also a member of a prominent family that had been impoverished and decimated during the Revolution. They married in 1797; the couple was only able to return to France in 1808. After the Restoration of the monarchy in 1814, they embarked on something like the life they had seemed destined for at birth: the duke was given important functions at court, while his wife presided over a brilliant salon in their apartment in the Tuileries Palace.

It was in her salon that she first told the true story of a black child brought back from Senegal shortly before the Revolution by the chevalier of Boufflers (who had served as governor of the colony), whose aunt, the princess of Beauvau, raised the child along with the princess's two grandsons. The story was so successful that its initial audience encouraged Duras to put it in writing. Like the most illustrious women writers of the Old Regime, from Lafayette to de Staël, Duras first became celebrated for her display of intelligence and conversational brilliance in the salons and only subsequently moved from this semiprivate arena to the public literary marketplace.[1]

Duras went public with her literary production as gradually as possible. When *Ourika* was first published, in 1823, the title page carried neither an author's name nor a date. More important, the novel was privately printed—only between twenty-five and forty copies were issued. The book did not remain a virtual secret for long, however. At least four new editions and reprints appeared in 1824 alone. The second edition was released in three printings of one thousand copies each. It sold out so quickly that, scarcely a month later, two thousand additional copies were printed. Two other editions that same year—the first a pirated one, the second an edition published in French in Saint Petersburg—confirm that, in a few months, *Ourika* had gone from being a story told privately in Duras's salon to being one of the most widely circulated novels of the day, a true best-seller. The year 1824 also saw the performance of no fewer than four plays based on *Ourika* and the publication of two poems inspired by the novel. Baron François-Pascal-Simon Gérard, court painter to Louis XVIII, made Duras's heroine the subject of a painting. *Ourika* was clearly one of those rare works that touch nerves acutely enough to become national obsessions.²

Duras's first novel is the story of a black child rescued from slavery and brought to France who believes herself to be like the aristocrats who raise her until she discovers racial difference and racial prejudice. This plot would hardly seem to be the stuff commercial dreams were made of in the France of 1824. Virtually from the beginning of its colonialist enterprise, France had instituted the most intricate official policy on race ever devised by a European nation. The earliest version of the Code Noir (the Black Code, or set of laws governing the status of slaves) was signed into effect by Louis XIV at Versailles in 1685. From then throughout the eighteenth century, the code was frequently reissued. The document became more specific in each revision, as legislators worked to close loopholes that gave some slaves rights and freedoms.

No questions inspired more obsessive rewriting than the interrelated specters of interracial marriage and the freeing of slaves. Whereas, for example, the original document provides that if a free white man in the colonies marries a slave woman, she is automatically freed, the 1711 version introduces laws forbidding interracial marriage (and therefore eliminating one means by which slaves theoretically could be freed). A last means of escape still remained, however: a slave brought to France by his or her master became free. Even this loophole was gradually closed by measures introduced in revisions of the code issued between 1716 and 1762. Finally, in 1777, the king forbade access to France to any "Black, mulatto, or other person of color," on the grounds that "negroes are multiplying every day in France" and that, as a result, "their marriages with Europeans are becoming more frequent" and "bloodlines are being altered" (Sala-Molins 220).[3]

During the Revolution, laws were introduced to grant equal rights to freed slaves. However, as soon as the French learned of the slave insurrection and the massacre of settlers in Santo Domingo (among the most repressive colonial regimes) in 1791, the fledgling French abolitionist movement was all but wiped out. A law abolishing slavery (although not the slave trade) was passed in 1794 but never went into effect; the Code Noir was reimposed in 1802 and reaffirmed in 1805.

The French abolitionist movement had returned to life in the decade before *Ourika*'s publication, and the new abolitionists were particularly active in the early 1820s (Daget 530–31). Against that background of controversy, we can best measure the novel's audacity. Not only was Duras's heroine brought to France after the law forbidding the country to all people of color had gone into effect; once there, Ourika proceeded to live out the very scenarios that French law had been attempting to ward off for a century and a half: she believes herself the equal of the French and even dares to fall in love with one of them.

It is astonishing that the French public—a public that had been exposed to little dialogue about slavery other than the Code Noir's ever-wilder fantasies of the black threat to French racial purity—would make *Ourika* a resounding commercial success. It is hardly less astonishing that such a story could have been produced under the Restoration and by someone surrounded by members of the court of Louis XVIII and the most prominent newly returned aristocratic émigrés. For in today's terminology Duras's milieu would be called not only the Right but the extreme Right—"the whitest of all white worlds," in John Fowles's apt characterization (*Ourika* [Austin: Taylor, 1977] 64). *Ourika*'s success is amazing; it is also a tribute to Duras's successful manipulation of public opinion on behalf of the newly regrouped abolitionist movement.

Even more remarkable than Duras's decision to treat this subject is the manner in which she did so. Previous portrayals of Africans in the French tradition are timid and vague. Olympe de Gouges's *L'esclavage des noirs ou l'heureux naufrage* (1789) and de Staël's *Mirza* (1795) seem contrived, humanitarian efforts: the black characters introduced are used to provoke reflection on the plight of slaves; they are not seen as individuals with psychological depth.[4] When *Ourika* is compared with these works, its originality and its author's daring are evident.

With Ourika, the first black heroine in a novel set in Europe and the first black female narrator in French literature, Duras created an African character who is truly an individual and not simply a type. The novel is, in Fowles's words, the "first serious attempt by a white novelist to enter a black mind" (xxxii). Ourika comes into her knowledge of herself through a powerful confrontation with her *négritude* (to borrow the classic term, made famous by Aimé Césaire and Léopold Senghor, for the development of racial consciousness), a confrontation that, in Duras's portrayal, is above all painful. From this point on, Ourika lives her life primarily not as a woman but as a black woman. After Ourika's awakening to her racial difference, all essential experience reaches her through the filter of her racial consciousness. She obsessively veils and covers any exposed skin, driven by the constant awareness that the simple fact of her color irrevocably separates her from the French society to which she had originally felt she belonged. With Ourika, Duras created a heroine designed more than anything to make the experience of prejudice as it is endured by its victim, and especially as it was endured on French soil, a reality for the French public of 1823. It seems hardly surprising that the French colonists on islands like Duras's mother's native Martinique were said to have been outraged by the novel's publication (Hoffmann 225).

Indeed, in the intricate political context in which she sets Ourika's tale, Duras includes only one element that could have made her novel's placement more palatable to the vast conservative public of her day. Very few previous literary works depicted life during revolutionary times—de Staël's *Delphine* (1802) is a notable exception—because censorship under all successive regimes had rendered the subject taboo. Duras, however, evokes the day-to-day existence of those aristocrats who had chosen to live out the Revolution on French soil. And, whereas de Staël chooses prudently to end her novel's action in September 1792, just before the outbreak of the Revolution's most extreme violence, Duras has Ourika tell us how the aristocratic circle she lived in experienced the full span of the Revolution, even the Terror.

Yet *Ourika*'s portrayal of revolutionary violence is complicated by its heroine's racial consciousness. In the paragraph before Ourika starts to evoke the beginning of the Terror, she describes her reactions to two events central to the French history of slavery: the official debate about the freeing of slaves (which inspires in Ourika the

realization that there are others like her) and the massacre of whites by slaves in Santo Domingo (which adds
to her shame because she then feels that she belongs to
"a race of barbarous murderers"[21]).

Duras's novel may be thought of as a web of contra-
dictions: a masterpiece of abolitionist literature that also
compares the suffering of slaves with that of aristocrats
during the Revolution; a work presenting the first fully
drawn black character in European literature who is ultimately destroyed by the very range and intensity of her
emotional responses—by her compassion for all those
who suffer, regardless of race, class, or gender, as much
as by her unrequited love for a white aristocrat. That the
novel is built on unresolved and unresolvable contradic-
tions makes *Ourika* the ideal lens through which to view
France in the early 1820s—a country that had known a
series of wildly different forms of government in the previous thirty-odd years, a country still emerging from the
horrors of the Revolution, a nation with a long struggle
ahead over its official racial policy.

Slavery finally became illegal in the French colonies
in 1848.

*Joan DeJean*
*University of Pennsylvania*

———◆———

In 1822, the duchess of Duras, ill and depressed, retreated
from Parisian court life and the company of her husband
to her country estate. There, at age forty-five, and in the
space of one extraordinary year, she drafted five novels,

among them *Ourika*. The wealthy Duras was clearly not writing for money, nor, she insisted to the elite inner circle to whom she read her manuscripts, was she writing for fame. Given prejudices at the time against women writers, her professed desire for privacy is hardly surprising. Nevertheless, Duras *did* finally make her writing public.

Duras's first work, *Ourika*, appeared in a limited private edition in 1823, and two years later her second novel, *Edouard*, was published in a similar format. Though no name appeared on the title pages, the socially prominent author's identity was an open secret, which perhaps helped fuel the demand for many more editions of both works. Meanwhile, however, rhymed verse mocking Duras's literary pretensions began making the rounds in Restoration social circles. Furthermore, although middle-class male writers such as Stendhal praised Duras's work in the press, they resented her success and social status and accused the author of affectation and vanity. When word spread about the audacious idea for Duras's third work of fiction—male impotence—Stendhal and his friend Henri de Latouche wrote anonymous novels on that subject and published *Armance* (1827) and *Olivier* (1829) in a similar format to pass off their work as hers and capitalize on her fame. Duras never published her third novel or any of her other works of fiction, and the public scandal created by Latouche's and Stendhal's impostures may have played a role in her silence. Until the republication of Duras's works in the 1970s, references to her fiction were found only in the footnotes of the Romantic canon, which is considered to have begun with *René* (1802), a novel by François-René de Chateaubriand, Duras's close friend and political protégé.[5]

In the countless Romantic works inspired by *René*, the protagonist is portrayed as an alienated genius alone with his melancholic thoughts. In Duras's *Ourika*, however, the French Romantic hero is from Africa, and she is black. Indeed, Duras's novel demonstrates that feminized and debilitated as male heroes were by the famous *mal du siècle*, or malaise of the age, they still enjoyed the privileges of upper-class white men.[6] Whereas in traditional Romantic novels, the heroes' predisposition to self-absorption and solitude excludes them from society, for Ourika, it is society that imposes her marginalization. As a woman living in the eighteenth century and as a young girl bought out of slavery and given to a noblewoman in France, Ourika derives her sense of self from her value as an object of social exchange and from the tenuous identity she creates for herself as a subject. The traditional Romantic hero flees society and roams aimlessly in search of a home he will never find. Ourika, by contrast, lacks the prerogative of mobility. Her social exclusion instead produces a paralyzing sense of psychological alienation that wreaks havoc not only on her soul but also on her body.

Narrated by that modern representative of secular authority—a doctor—*Ourika* is one of the earliest examples of the pathologizing of emotion in literature, and her symptoms as well as their "cure" are now classic. Severely depressed, Ourika is also feverish, insomniac, and excessively thin. "It's the past we must cure . . .," the doctor decides. "But to do that, I must know it first" (5). In her conversations with him, however, Ourika declares that she cannot remember her African past and that France, "this land of exile" (39), is the only home she has known.

Brought there at age two, she has made herself and been made in the image of the privileged Enlightenment society that took her in. She describes her childhood as an idyllic blur, dissolving the distinctions between herself and Mme de B., her solicitous adoptive mother, as well as Mme de B.'s grandson, Charles, whom she sees as her brother. So complete is her assimilation that she even feels "a sharp contempt for everything that [doesn't] belong in that world" (8).

Once she is old enough to circulate in the marriage market, however, Ourika discovers in one searing moment that her blissful integration is an illusion: the only white man who might consent to have mulatto children would be a social inferior interested in Ourika's dowry. Thus barred by racial prejudice from a young heroine's ultimate rite of passage—love and marriage—Ourika instantly sees herself as the other: "always alone in the world. And never loved!" (16). As a result of this painful enlightenment, Ourika learns not only to "analyz[e] and criticiz[e] almost all that had previously satisfied [her]" (17) but also to call into question the so-called "natural order of things" (14) and the universality of the supreme Enlightenment value: reason. "But who can say what is or isn't rational?" she asks. "Is reason the same for everyone?" (27). In sharp contrast with almost all other early Romantic protagonists, Duras's heroine notes the specific social, historical, and political causes of her alienation and makes her story a vehicle for pointed social criticism. Thus, for Ourika, the "great chaos" (19) brought about by the French Revolution provides a glimpse of a society reorganized according to principles of real equality, where she might find her rightful place. Soon after, however, Ourika sees in the violent opinions stirred by the Revolution only unenlightened self-interest—"exaggerations, conceits, fears" (20)—and denounces and fears the social and political upheaval the Revolution had set in motion.

While most Romantic heroes find in alienation proof of their superiority, Ourika desires equality and makes a claim for it on the basis of her similarity to others, not her difference from them. Nevertheless, French racial prejudices instill in her a self-hatred that makes her body, and her skin in particular, an object of revulsion to her. In a desperate attempt to remain unseen, she removes all the mirrors from her room. At a time when women in French high society exposed themselves in transparent white muslin gowns revealing equally pale skin, Ourika tells the doctor: "I wore gloves all the time, and dresses that hid my neck and arms. When I went out of doors, I put on a large hat with a veil. I even wore it indoors frequently" (28). By the time the doctor meets her, she has donned a long black veil and chosen the seclusion of the convent. Nevertheless, there is no escape from the other's "sneering face," precisely because she has internalized that gaze: "I saw it in my dreams, in every waking moment. It stood before me like my own reflection" (29).

When openly confronted by Mme de B.'s friend, the marquise, who insists on knowing the cause of Ourika's distress, the heroine is fierce in her own defense: "I have no secret, Madame. You know very well what my problems are. My social situation. And the color of my skin" (42). The marquise insists, however, that Ourika's problem is not society's racism but her unreciprocated passion for Charles, who is in love with someone else. Although Ourika strongly protests her innocence, she begins to wonder whether she is in fact guilty of illicit passion. Later Ourika defends her feelings for Charles as the unselfish love of a sister or mother, but her last words in the text identify the convent as the "one place where [she] may still think of [Charles] day and night . . ." (46). By adding the complication of a love thwarted by social obstacles to the life story on which the novel is based, Duras follows the pattern of Romantic novels that use a love interest to heighten the pathos of the protagonist's situation. The introduction of romance makes the heroine's psychological dilemma even more complex, but at the same time it blunts the novel's social and political criticism precisely in the areas—gender and race—where *Ourika* departs most radically from the Romantic tradition.

As with most female protagonists, Ourika's horizon is limited by society's definitions of a woman's place and role. The far more explicitly feminist heroines of earlier novels like Françoise de Graffigny's *Lettres d'une Péruvienne* (1747) and de Staël's *Corinne* (1807) bridle against these restrictions and openly call them into question, but Ourika instead strongly protests her unjust exclusion from love and marriage. So great is her desire to have a family and be among her own people that she claims at one moment that she would prefer the horrors of slavery to her current status as outsider: "I might now have been the black slave of some rich planter[.] Scorched by the sun, I should be laboring on someone else's land. But I should have a poor hut of my own to go to at day's end; a partner in my life, children of my own race" (39). Such a remark makes vivid the pain caused by "benevolent" paternalism and racial prejudice. Later, however, Ourika, who claims she felt a sympathetic affinity with the African slaves of

Santo Domingo, says that once she heard they had risen up in violent revolt she condemned them as "a race of barbarous murderers" (21). Ourika's denunciation of the 1791 slave revolts is a far cry from the support that some white sympathizers of the time had declared for the rebellion. Does setting up slavery as a desirable alternative to marginalization diminish its horror, which abolitionists were attempting to impress on the public at the time the novel was published?

Duras's Senegalese heroine, raised, educated, and thoroughly socialized in France, is thus even more conservative than some of her white contemporaries. Identifying with the white society that excludes her, Ourika experiences her blackness as a kind of incurable malady to which she is ultimately resigned (Hoffmann 224). Desperately ill at the beginning of the doctor's frame narrative, Ourika claims nevertheless that she is happy. Rejecting the secular values of Mme de B. and her circle, Ourika has found consolation in religion, a remedy to her dilemma that would have been particularly palatable to Duras's readers during the Restoration. Naming faith in a color-blind God as the source of her newfound resignation, she condemns her own distress and she dies soon after, "with the last of the autumn leaves" (47).

In *Ourika*, the outsider whose difference makes her critical of French society also serves as its spokesperson, a mirroring the heroine identifies as both pleasurable and demeaning. Though she acknowledges that she was loved, spoiled, and praised, she asserts that she was also for Mme de B. and her friends "a toy, an amusement" (12) that reassured them of their supposed lack of prejudice. Until she finally decides to speak to the doctor, Ourika confides in no one, not even Mme de B., because, she says, "You confide in people—then they tell you it was your own fault" (6). This comment suggests that even the narrative Ourika tells the doctor may not be, perhaps never could be, the whole story. Indeed, it is not she but the doctor who records, edits, and frames her words. Most important of all, Ourika is not the eighteenth-century African woman whose story originally inspired the work but a fiction created by the duchess of Duras in the 1820s. Is race in the novel used by Duras as a metaphor and "cure" for her own sense of alienation?[7]

Whatever the author's explicit intentions or unconscious motivations, the choices Duras made had and continue to have complex effects. Making the Romantic hero a woman, *Ourika* highlights the key role that gender plays in the representation of the alienated Romantic protagonist. Making her black as well, the novel shows race as a social construction and vigorously protests the injustices to which it gives rise. Despite its layers of narrative embedding and "othering," or perhaps precisely because of the complexities that result, *Ourika* uses Romantic empathy to shed new light on Enlightenment values and raises a multitude of questions: When and how is paternalism a form of cruelty? What combination of forces prevented Ourika from protesting injustice more explicitly before she retreated from the world? What made this story about the unthinking cruelty of upper-class white society so popular with that very society in the 1820s? And, finally, what will readers make of it today?

*Margaret Waller*
*Pomona College*

# Notes

[1] When she moved from oral to written narration, Duras considerably expanded the true story on which *Ourika* was based. The child raised in the Hôtel de Beauvau (which now houses the French Ministry of the Interior) died when she was only sixteen.

[2] The obsession with *Ourika* even crossed national borders. For example, in 1826 Goethe wrote Alexander von Humboldt (who told Duras of the letter) that he had been "overwhelmed" by the novel (cited by Scheler 28n30).

[3] It is estimated that during the entire eighteenth century no more than one thousand to five thousand slaves reached French soil—hardly the "prodigious quantity" evoked by the 1777 Code Noir (Sala-Molins 220).

[4] I use the vocabulary that is more or less the equivalent in today's American English of the racial terminology chosen by Duras. In France in 1824, the most progressive usage referred to slaves as *noirs* (blacks). However, when Duras speaks of *nègres* and *négresses*, she is using a terminology that was not at all pejorative then, one that was still used by most abolitionists in their official speeches and one that would have been the only standard usage in the late eighteenth century, in which her novel is set. On the history of the French vocabulary of race, see Daget; and Delesalle and Valensi. Daget shows in particular both how politically charged and how unstable usage was: for instance, after the 1791 massacres in Santo Domingo, the term *noir* suddenly almost ceased to be used (535).

[5] Denise Virieux's, Grant Critchfield's, and Claudine Herrmann's works brought Duras to the attention of modern scholars; John Fowles's first English translation of *Ourika* appeared around the same time.

[6] For more on the differences between male and female authors' treatment of the *mal du siècle*, see Waller.

[7] See Pailhès; Herrmann; and Bertrand-Jennings.

## WORKS BY
# Claire de Duras

*Ourika* (1823). Published anonymously.

*Edouard* (1825). Published anonymously. Ed. Gérard Gengembre. Paris: Autrement, 1994.

*Pensées de Louis XIV extraites de ses ouvrages et de ses lettres manuscrites*. Paris: L. Passard, 1827.

### Posthumous Works

*Le frère ange* (1829). Anonymous.

*Réflexions et prières inédites*. Paris: Debécourt, 1839.

*Olivier, ou le secret*. Ed. Denise Virieux. Paris: José Corti, 1971.

### Unpublished Works

"Les mémoires de Sophie"

"Le moine, ou l'abbé du Mont Saint-Bernard"

# SUGGESTIONS FOR FURTHER READING

Bertrand-Jennings, Chantal. "Condition féminine et impuissance sociale: Les romans de la duchesse de Duras." *Romantisme* 63 (1989): 39–50.

Crichfield, Grant. *Three Novels by Mme de Duras: Ourika, Edouard, Olivier.* The Hague: Mouton, 1975.

Daget, Serge. "Les mots esclave, nègre, Noir, et les jugements de valeur sur la traite négrière dans la littérature abolitionniste française de 1770 à 1845." *Revue française d'histoire d'outre-mer* 60 (1973): 511–48.

Delesalle, Simone, and Lucette Valensi. "Le mot 'nègre' dans les dictionnaires français d'ancien régime: Histoire et lexicographie." *Langue française* 15 (Sept. 1972): 79–104.

Herrmann, Claudine. Introduction. *Ourika.* By Claire de Duras. Paris: Femmes, 1979. 7–22.

Hoffmann, Léon-François. *Le nègre romantique: Personnage littéraire et obsession collective.* Paris: Payot, 1973.

Kadish, Doris, and Françoise Massardier-Kenney. *Translating Slavery: Gender and Race in French Women's Writing, 1783–1823.* Kent: Kent State UP, 1994.

Little, Roger. Presentation. *Ourika.* By Claire de Duras. Ed. Little. U of Exeter P, 1993. 27–67.

O'Connell, David. "*Ourika*: Black Face, White Mask." *French Review* 47 (1974): 47–56.

Pailhès, Abbé Gabriel. *La Duchesse de Duras et Chateaubriand d'après des documents inédits*. Paris: Perrin, 1910.

Sala-Molins, Louis. *Le Code Noir, ou, le Calvaire de Canaan*. Paris: PU de France, 1987.

Scheler, Lucien. "Un best-seller sous Louis XVIII: *Ourika* de Mme de Duras." *Bulletin du bibliophile* 1 (1988): 11–28.

Switzer, Richard. "Mme de Staël, Mme de Duras, and the Question of Race." *Kentucky Romance Quarterly* 20 (1973): 303–16.

Virieux, Denise. Introduction. *Olivier, ou le secret*. By Claire de Duras. Paris: Corti, 1971. 14–124.

Waller, Margaret. *The Male Malady: Fictions of Impotence in the French Romantic Novel*. New Brunswick: Rutgers UP, 1993.

# FOREWORD

Everyone knows that writers need understanding agents
and editors at the beginning of their careers. I suspect
they almost equally require understanding booksellers. I
was lucky in that respect, since I ran across Mr. Francis
Norman and his antiquarian bookshop in Hampstead,
London, and learned a great deal more about literature
there than I ever did at Oxford.

Let me hazard a definition of what this kind of bookshop should be like. It must be run by a person of humor,
learning, and curiosity, to whom nothing in book form
is alien, who will show you an Elzevir title page one
moment and read you a passage from a sci-fi paperback
the next. It should be kept in a permanent state of appar-
ent chaos—always too many books for the shelf space,
always piles and boxes of new-bought lots awaiting
inspection. Above all, it must be catholic in its offerings,
because its prime function for young writers is to help
them realize their tastes—even to the extreme of convincing them that they don't like old books at all.

What we learn at university is to appreciate the prescribed masterpieces; we never have time to explore that
vast bulk of the iceberg beneath the examination surface.

I left Oxford in a state of total confusion as to my real (as opposed to my acquired) tastes in literature. And it wasn't until I began to frequent Mr. Norman's and its presiding spirit—now both dead, alas—that I discovered what I was as a bookman. It was partly the choice, the gamble, the delight of the unexpected; the realization that there were other ways of loving and being erudite about books than the academic; perhaps it was above all, in those days, never having very much money to spend. The rich may suit their smallest fancies. The poor get to know what they really like.

I regret bitterly the general disappearance of such shops from the Britain (and, I am told, the America) of the 1990s. It is partly, of course, a matter of inflation and scarcity. Not even my friend Mr. Norman could now leave minor seventeenth- and eighteenth-century volumes, coverless and dog-eared, lying about for sale at giveaway prices to whoever unearths them. The great country-house sources have dried up, the demands and funds of university librarians the world over seem endless. But I was the other day in one of the largest secondhand bookstores in Britain: a colossal stock, all neatly shelved, cataloged and unbargainably high-priced, briskly efficient assistants at every turn. Such establishments may be a librarian's, a research scholar's dream. I could only weep for those two dusty, overcrowded rooms in Hampstead, where nothing could ever be found at once and somehow everything turned up in the end. The one place makes bibliophily seem a coldly calculated science; the other, a love affair.

My particular affair with the strange little novel that follows began some thirty-two years ago in Mr. Norman's.

OURIKA, said the title page. *Paris, 1824.* There was no indi-cation of author, I had never heard of the book, the copy was badly foxed, and I didn't anticipate much reward for the five shillings, then one dollar, I paid for it. If I paid even that it was simply on the strength of a glance at the open-ing sentence. One of the things I learned in that shop is that I adore narrative, real or imagined. It has become for me the quintessence of the novelist's art—and I liked the feel of the immediate bald plunge into story of *Ourika.* But I thought I would be disappointed, that I had lum-bered myself with one more insipid nouvelle in the Mar-montel tradition—some piece of didactic morality tinged with a dilute Romanticism, and a wasted buy even to someone with my inveterately magpie attitude to book collecting. I took the little octavo, green marbled-paper covers, quarter-bound in worn black calf, home and sat down to prove my fear right. Long before I had finished, I knew I had stumbled on a minor masterpiece.

I reread it almost at once and have done so a number of times again over the years. If anything, my admiration for *Ourika* has grown, and grown more than I realized. I chose the name of the hero in my own novel *The French Lieutenant's Woman* quite freely—or so I thought at the time. It came as a shock, months after my typescript had gone to the printers, to pick up *Ourika* one day and to recall that Charles was the name of the principal male figure there also. That set me thinking. And though I could have sworn I had never had the African figure of Ourika herself in mind during the writing of *The French Lieutenant's Woman,* I am now certain in retrospect that she was very active in my unconscious.

Oddly enough I had been more than normally self-aware of the origins of my own novel during the course of its writing, since I had promised to contribute to an anthology called *Afterwords* (Harper and Row, 1969), in which a number of us were to try to explain how we came to write our books. I explained in my own contribution how the seed of mine had come in a half-waking dream and consisted of an image of a woman standing with her back to me. She was in black, and her stance had a disturbing mixture of both rejection and accusation. Another characteristic of this image had been its refusal to "move" into the present. I was clear that I wanted to write about a woman who had been unfairly exiled from society. But I've never liked historical novels and had no desire to write one. It took me some months to accept that this ghostly presence adamantly refused to become contemporary. Today I do not understand how I can have been so stupid as not to see who that woman really was. I'm afraid it has revealed to me a remnant of color prejudice, since something in my unconscious cheated on the essential clue. The woman in my mind who would not turn had black clothes but a white face.

However, the last thing I want to do is to offer this present translation as a footnote to my own work. Englishing it has been a labor of love, no labor at all, and publishing it is an act of homage to a forgotten writer.

I should like to say one other thing about this first serious attempt by a white novelist to enter a black mind. I suppose a certain kind of contemporary black extremist might dismiss Ourika's story with a sneer—given the basic inauthenticity of her position, she deserves everything that comes to her. Such a sneer is, of course, historically ridiculous. By such standards, we should have to blame Columbus for taking so long to cross the Atlantic, when he could have done it by air in a few hours. There were only two choices, in the Europe of 1780–1805, the period *Ourika* spans, for an African *woman*: she could be an ignorant slave or she could be a social leper.

Ourika may cut a poor figure as an early Black Panther; but she is convincing as an intelligent human being, intolerably torn between her *négritude* and her European-educated mind. Many African writers, both French- and English-speaking, have since analyzed that particular predicament, and the countless black American fictional and biographical treatments of the problem need no mention here. Yet I doubt if the essence of the situation, the basic tragic equation, has ever been put more neatly and simply than in this little book. An added virtue, at least in my eyes, is that it universalizes the particular racial context, goes just as well for any intelligent member of a despised minority in a jealous and blind majority culture. Indeed it touches on one of the deepest chords in all art, the despair of ever attaining freedom in a determined and determining environment; and this is why if in one way *Ourika* has its roots in the French seventeenth century, in Racine, La Rochefoucauld, and Mme de Lafayette, in another it reaches forward to the age of Sartre and Camus. This is the case history of an outsider, of the eternal *étranger* in human society.

*John Fowles, 1994*

### Note

This foreword is a revised version of the foreword written for the translation published in 1977.

# A WORD ABOUT THE TRANSLATION

This translation is a slightly revised version of Fowles's previous English translation of *Ourika*, which was published in a limited edition by W. Thomas Taylor in 1977. The Modern Language Association thanks the Fales Library at New York University and Maxime La Fantasie, assistant librarian, for making this edition available.

CLAIRE DE DURAS


# Ourika


*This is to be alone, this,*
*this is solitude!*
                    *—Byron*

*The Doctor*

# Introduction

*A few months after I had finished my medical studies at Mont-*
*pellier and begun practicing in Paris, I was called one morning*
*to a convent in the Faubourg Saint Jacques to see a young nun*
*who was ill. Napoleon, by then emperor, had recently sanctioned*
*the reestablishment of some of the convents. The one to which I*
*had to go belonged to the Ursuline order and devoted itself to*
*teaching the young. Part of the building had been destroyed dur-*
*ing the Revolution, and the demolition of the ancient church, of*
*which no more than a few vault arches remained, left the clois-*
*ters open on one side.*

*It was to these cloisters that I was conducted by a sister. I*
*noticed, as we went through them, that the long flagstones with*
*which they were paved were in fact tombstones, since they bore*
*inscriptions, though most had become illegible with age. Some*
*had been broken during the Revolution, and the sister remarked*
*that they had not yet had time to have them repaired. I had*
*never before seen the inside of a convent, and it was therefore*
*an entirely new experience for me.*

*From the cloisters we passed into the garden, where the sick*
*nun had been carried; and there she was, sitting at the end of a*
*long hedged path, almost entirely hidden by her large black veil.*

*"Here is the doctor," said my guide, and withdrew.*

*I approached a little nervously. The sight of the tombstones*
*had chilled me and I imagined I was about to meet a new victim*
*of the convent system. The anticlerical prejudices of my early*

years had been reawakened; and my concern for the woman I was to treat rose in sympathy with my views on the kind of injustice I supposed her to have suffered. She turned toward me. I had a strange shock. I was looking at a negress.

I very soon found myself even further surprised by her welcoming grace of manner and the elegant simplicity of her language.

"You've been called to see a very sick person," she said. "I do want to be cured now. But it hasn't always been so, and perhaps that is the real cause of my illness."

I asked for her symptoms.

"I experience a constant feeling of being weighed down," she said. "I can't sleep anymore. And I have a persistent fever."

Her appearance only too exactly confirmed this unpromising syndrome. She was excessively thin. The sole things that gave light to her face were her extraordinarily large and luminous eyes and her dazzlingly white teeth. Her mind still lived, but her body was destroyed. She showed every sign of having suffered from prolonged and acute melancholia.

Touched more than I could say, I resolved to try to save her, and began by telling her that she must calm her imagination, think of other things, push away all painful memories.

"But I'm happy now. I've never known such peace and contentment."

There was a sincerity of tone, a gentleness in her voice that made disbelief impossible. My astonishment grew.

"You certainly haven't always thought that. I can see you have suffered—and over a long period."

4

*"I can't deny it," she replied. "I found peace of mind very late. But now, I am happy."*

*"Well then, if that's the case, it's the past we must cure. Let us hope we can. But to do that, I must know it first."*

*"It is full of extravagances."*

*She spoke sadly, on the brink of tears.*

*"And you say you are happy now!"*

*But there was no hesitation in her reply. "I am happy now. And so self-reconciled that not even the promise of all I once longed to be could tempt me to change my present existence. I have no secrets. The story of my unhappiness is the same as the story of my life. I suffered so much, before I came here, that my health was slowly ruined. My future held no hope, I was glad to feel myself dying. That was an unforgivable longing. And you see how I've been punished for it. Now that I want to live, it may be too late."*

*I comforted her and gave her hopes of a quick recovery. But even as I murmured consoling words and promised her life, some dark presentiment warned me that it was too late. Death had marked down its victim.*

*I saw this young nun several times more. She seemed touched by the concern I showed for her, and one day returned of her own free will to the subject of her past.*

*"The miseries of my life must seem so peculiar that I've always been very reluctant to talk about them. No one can gauge*

how much another has suffered. You confide in people—then they tell you it was your own fault."

"I would never do that. I can see the terrible effects of unhappiness too clearly to doubt your sincerity."

"But you will doubt my reason."

"Even if I did—does such a doubt exclude sympathy?"

"It generally does. But if you really can't cure me unless you know the troubles that have ruined my health . . . then I will tell you about them when we know each other a little better."

I visited the convent more and more frequently. The treatment I had prescribed seemed not without some effect. Finally, one day last summer, I found her alone in the same arbor and on the same bench as during my first visit. We took up our previous conversation. She told me what follows.

# Ourika

I was brought here from Senegal when I was two years old by the Chevalier de B., who was then governor there. One day he saw me being taken aboard a slaver that was soon to leave port. My mother had died and in spite of my cries I was being carried to the ship. He took pity and bought me and then, when he returned to France, gave me to his aunt, Mme la Maréchale de B. She was one of the most attractive women of her time, combining a fine mind with a very genuine warmth of heart.

Rescued from slavery, placed under the protection of Mme de B.—it was as if my life had been twice saved. I have shown ingratitude to Providence by being so unhappy since. But does understanding bring happiness? I suspect the reverse is true. The privileges of knowledge have to be bought at the cost of the consolations of ignorance. The myth doesn't say whether Galatea was given happiness as well as life.

I didn't learn of the circumstances of my earliest childhood till long afterward. My first memories are of Mme de B.'s drawing room. I spent my life there, loved by her, fondled, spoiled by all her friends, loaded with presents, praised, held up as the most clever and endearing of children.

The chief characteristic of her circle was enthusiasm, but it was an enthusiasm governed by good taste and hostile to all excess. One praised all that might be praised; and one excused all that might be blamed. Often, by a charming mental sleight of hand, a person's defects were transformed into virtues. Popularity brings boldness of judgment and with Mme de B. one was as highly valued as one could be—perhaps overvalued, since without realizing it she lent something of her own character to her friends. Watching her, listening to her, people began to feel they resembled her.

Dressed in oriental costume, seated at her feet, I used to listen—long before I could understand it—to the conversation of the most distinguished men of the day. I had none of the usual boisterousness of children. I was thoughtful before I could think, and I was content to be at her side. For me "to love" meant to be there, to hear her talk, to obey her—above all, to watch her. I wanted no more of life. I couldn't marvel at my living in the lap of luxury, at my being surrounded by grace and intelligence, because I knew no other way of life. But without realizing it, I acquired a sharp contempt for everything that didn't belong in that world. *My* world. To possess good taste is like having perfect pitch in music. Even as a small child, bad taste offended me. I could sense it before I could define it, and habit made good taste an essential requirement of my life. Such a demand would have been dangerous, even if I'd had a future. But I had no future, though I was totally unaware of that then.

I reached the age of twelve without its once occurring to me that there might be other ways of being happy besides mine. I didn't regret being black. I was told I was an angel. There was nothing to warn me that the color of my skin might be a disadvantage. I saw very few other children. I had only one friend of my own age and my dark skin never meant he did not like me.

My benefactress had two grandsons, children of a daughter who had died young. The younger brother, Charles, was about the same age as myself. Brought up beside me, he was my champion, adviser, and defender in all my small misdemeanors. He went away to school when he was seven and the tears I shed when he was leaving were my first sorrow. I used to think of him a great deal, but I no longer saw him except at rare intervals. He studied. And I for my part learned, to please Mme de B., all that is considered essential for a girl's perfect education.

She wanted me to be accomplished at everything. I had a good voice and was trained by the best singing masters. I liked painting, and a famous painter, a friend of Mme de B.'s, took it upon himself to direct my efforts. I learned English and Italian and Mme de B. herself made sure I was well read. She guided my intellect and formed my judgment. When I talked with her and discovered the treasures of her mind, I felt my own exalted. It was admiration for her that opened my own intelligence to me. Alas, I didn't know then that these innocent studies would ripen into such bitter fruit. I thought only of pleasing her. All my future was a smile of approval on her lips.

However, my extensive reading, especially of poetry, began to exercise my young imagination. I had no goal in life, no plan, so I allowed my thoughts to wander where they would. With the naïve self-confidence of my age, I told myself that Mme de B. would certainly find a way to make me happy. Her fondness for me, the kind of life I was leading, everything prolonged my mistaken view of existence and made my blindness natural.

Let me give you an example of the attention and favor I was accorded. Today perhaps, you'll find it hard to believe that I was considered once to have a fashionably beautiful figure. Mme de B. often praised what she called my natural grace and she had had me taught to dance to perfection. To show this talent of mine to the world she gave a ball—ostensibly for her grandsons, but really to display me, much to my advantage, in a quadrille symbolizing the four corners of the globe. I was to represent Africa. Travelers were asked for advice, books of costumes were ransacked, and learned tomes on African music consulted. At last a *comba*—the national dance of my country—was chosen. My partner covered his face in a mask of black crepe, a disguise I did not need. I say that sadly now. But at the time, it meant nothing to me.

I threw myself into the pleasures of the ball and danced the *comba* with all the success one might expect

10

from so novel a spectacle. The audience were for the most part friends of Mme de B. and they thought the warmer their applause, the more she would be pleased. But the dance was in any case something fresh and different. It consisted of stately steps broken by various poses, describing love, grief, triumph, and despair. I was totally ignorant of such violent emotions, but some instinct taught me how to mimic their effects. In short, I triumphed. I was applauded, surrounded, overwhelmed with congratulations. It was unalloyed pleasure. Still nothing troubled my sense of security.

But a few days after the ball, a chance-heard conversation dropped the scales from my eyes and ended my childhood.

There was, in Mme de B.'s drawing room, a large lacquer screen. It was meant to hide a door, but it also reached as far as one of the windows—and there, between the window and the screen, was a table where I used sometimes to draw. One day I was taking great care over a miniature I had almost finished. Absorbed in what I was doing, I'd sat motionless for some time, and no doubt Mme de B. thought I had left the room. One of her friends was announced.

She was a certain marquise, a bleakly practical lady with an incisive mind, and frank to the point of dryness. She was like this even with her friends. She would do anything for them, but she made them pay dearly for her concern on their behalf. Inquisitorial and persistent, her demands were matched only by her sense of duty. She was the least agreeable of Mme de B.'s circle and though she was kind to me in her fashion, I was afraid of her. When she interrogated you, even though it was with great severity, she meant well and to show her interest in you. But unfortunately I'd grown so accustomed to kinder methods that I was alarmed by her bluntness.

"Now that we're alone," said the marquise to Mme de B., "I must speak to you about Ourika. She's become a charming girl and her mind is mature. Soon she'll be able to converse as well as you. She's talented, unusual, has ease of manner. But what next? To come to the point—what do you intend doing with her?"

I heard Mme de B. sigh. "It's very much on my mind. And, I confess, sadly on my mind. I love her as if she were my own daughter. I'd do anything to make her happy. And yet—the more seriously I think about it, the further away a solution seems. I see the poor girl alone, always alone in the world."

I could never describe to you the effect those few words had on me. Lightning does not strike more swiftly. I comprehended all. I was black. Dependent, despised, without fortune, without resource, without a single other being of my kind to help me through life. All I had been until then was a toy, an amusement for my mistress; and soon I was to be cast out of a world that could never admit me. I was seized by a frightful trembling, everything grew dark, and for a moment the pounding of my heart prevented me from hearing more. At last I recovered enough to listen to the continuation of their conversation. The marquise was speaking.

"What concerns me is that you are making her future misery certain. What could please her now, having spent all her life close by your side?"

"But she will continue there!"

"Very well—so long as she remains a child. But she's fifteen already. To whom do you propose marrying her? With her intelligence, with the education you've given her? What kind of man would marry a negress? Even supposing you could bribe some fellow to father mulatto children, he could only be of low birth. She could never be happy with such a man. She can only want the kind of husband who would never look at her."

"I can't dispute all that," said Mme de B. "But mercifully she still knows nothing. And she has an affection for me that may save her from having to face reality for many years yet. To have made her happy I'd have had to try to turn her into a common servant. I sincerely believe that could never have been done. And who knows? Since she's too remarkable to be anything less than she is, perhaps one day she will rise above her fate."

"Wishful thinking!" snapped the marquise. "Reason may help people overcome bad luck. But it's powerless against evils that arise from deliberately upsetting the natural order of things. Ourika has flouted her natural destiny. She has entered society without its permission. It will have its revenge."

"But she's most obviously innocent of such a crime!" exclaimed Mme de B. "You're very hard on the poor child."

"I have her interests at heart more than you. I want her happiness, and you are destroying it."

Mme de B. answered with some heat, and I was about to become the cause of a quarrel between the two friends. But another visitor was announced. I slipped behind the screen and escaped from the room. I ran to my own. There a flood of tears temporarily relieved my swollen heart.

This loss of the till-then-unshaken sense of my own worth effected a profound change in my life. There are illusions like daylight. When they go, all becomes night. In the turmoil of new ideas that besieged me, I lost sight of everything that had engaged my mind in the past. It was a yawning gulf of horrors. I saw myself hounded by contempt, misplaced in society, destined to be the bride of some venal "fellow" who might condescend to get half-breed children on me. Such thoughts rose up one after the other like phantoms and fastened on me like furies. Above all, it was the isolation. Had I not heard it from Mme de B.'s own mouth—"alone, always alone in the world"? Again and again I repeated that phrase: alone, always alone. Only a day before, being alone had meant nothing. I knew nothing of loneliness, I had never felt it. I needed what I loved and it had never crossed my mind that what I loved did not need me in return. But now my eyes were opened, and my misfortune had already introduced mistrust into my heart.

When I went back to the drawing room, everyone was struck by my altered appearance. Questions were asked, I said I didn't feel well. I was taken at my word. Mme de B. sent for Doctor Barthez, who examined me carefully and took my pulse, and then announced curtly that I was fit as a fiddle. Her fears calmed, Mme de B. tried to take me out of myself by means of all sorts of amusements. I'm ashamed to tell you how ungrateful I was to her; my soul had crept back inside itself. The best kindnesses are those that touch deepest. But I was too full of resentment to be generous. Endless permutations of the same thoughts obsessed every hour of my day. They reproduced themselves in a thousand different shapes, and my imagination endowed them with the darkest colors. Often I passed whole nights weeping. All my pity was for myself.

My face revolted me, I no longer dared to look in a mirror. My black hands seemed like monkey's paws. I exaggerated my ugliness to myself, and this skin color of

15

mine seemed to me like the brand of shame. It exiled me from everyone else of my natural kind. It condemned me to be alone, always alone in the world. And never loved! For the price of a dowry, a fellow might consent to have mulatto children! My whole being rose in rage against that idea. I thought for a moment of asking Mme de B. to send me back to my homeland. But I would still have been alone. Who there could listen to me now, or understand me?

I no longer belonged anywhere. I was cut off from the entire human race.

It was not until long afterward that I saw how I might resign myself to such a fate. Mme de B. was not especially religious. What feelings of the kind I had myself I owed to a worthy priest who had prepared me for first communion. In keeping with my character, these feelings were sincere. But I hadn't grasped that faith is of little use unless it informs every action one takes. Mine had taken up a few minutes of each day, and had had nothing to do with the rest. My confessor was a saintly old man. But he never probed. I used to see him only two or three times a year. And since I considered unhappiness no sin, I told him nothing of my troubles.

They visibly affected my health, yet paradoxically improved my mind. A wise man of the East once said, "Who hasn't suffered, knows nothing." And I had known nothing before my bitter awakening, I'd seen everything in terms of feelings, I didn't judge, I simply liked. I thought of persons, actions, ways of talking as things that pleased or displeased me emotionally. But now my mind stood back from these instinctive reactions. Sorrow is a remoteness and bans one from appraising objects separately. From the time I felt ostracized, I became more exacting. I analyzed and criticized almost all that had previously satisfied me.

Mme de B. couldn't help noticing this change in my nature. I've never discovered whether she guessed the cause. Perhaps she felt that if she let me unburden my heart, it would make things worse. At any rate she was kinder to me than usual, talking to me with entire freedom. In an attempt to get me to forget my own woes, she started revealing her own. She had read my character well: I could feel in harmony with life only when I knew myself necessary, or at least useful, to her. What haunted me most was the notion that I was alone on earth, that I might die without being regretted by a single person. This was unkind to Mme de B., who loved me, and had abundantly proved it. But there were others she was more concerned for than me. I didn't envy the affection she lavished on her grandsons, especially on Charles. But I longed in vain for their privilege of being able to call her mother.

These bonds of family gave me a terrible insight into my own situation. I was never to be a sister, a wife, a mother myself. I dreamed such relationships to be far more pleasant than perhaps they are. And being unable to enjoy them, I disregarded those I could have known. I had no friend of my own sex and age, no one I could trust. What I felt for Mme de B. was more religious than emotional. But I believe I felt for Charles exactly as a sister.

He was still at school, though he was shortly to leave in order to travel with his elder brother and their tutor. They were to visit Germany, England, and Italy, and would be away for two years. Charles was delighted to be going, and I wasn't sad until the last moment—whatever pleased him had always pleased me as well. I'd said nothing of all the ideas that obsessed me. I never saw him alone, and it would have taken too long to have explained my wretched problems to him. I'm sure he would have understood, if I had done so. But in his gentle, grave way he had a tendency to make fun of people. This made me timid, even though sincerity disarmed him. He really laughed only at those who were ludicrously pretentious. In the end I said nothing. In any case his going away was a kind of distraction. I think it did me good to have something besides myself to be sad about.

Not long after the departure of Charles, the Revolution took a more serious turn. The sole topics of conversation in Mme de B.'s drawing room were the vast moral and political questions the Revolution had so profoundly posed, and that have exercised the minds of intelligent men since the beginning of time. Nothing was better calculated to widen and mold my ideas than hearing all this debated. Every day I listened to clever men reexamining what had till then been considered settled. They left nothing undissected, tracked every human institution back to its origins . . . though only too often they finally left everything undermined and destroyed.

Young as I was, ignorant of the intrinsic selfishness of society, nursing my secret wound in silence . . . you won't find it hard to believe that the Revolution brought a change in my views of life. It gave me a wisp of hope, and for a brief while I forgot my own problems. One is quick to grasp at any consolation, and I sensed that at the end of this great chaos I might find my true place. When personal destiny was turned upside down, all social caste overthrown, all prejudices had disappeared, a state of affairs might one day come to pass where I would feel myself less exiled. If I truly possessed some superiority of mind, some hidden quality, then it would be appreciated when my color no longer isolated me, as it had until then, in the heart of society. But it so happened that these very qualities that I saw in myself soon disabused me. I couldn't for long desire so much present evil for my own small future good.

Besides, I couldn't help remarking the ridiculousness of the men who were trying to control the course of events. I perceived the smallness of their characters, I guessed their real philosophies. I soon stopped being the dupe of their false notion of fraternity. Realizing that people still found time, in all this adversity, to despise me, I gave up hope.

For all that, I found the lively discussions constantly absorbing, until they lost what had been their greatest charm. Already the time when one thought only of pleasing, and when the first condition of success was to forget one's own vanity, was past. The moment the Revolution became something more than a fine theory and touched the private interests of the individual, the debates degenerated into quarrels. A sharpness, a sourness, a personal animosity took the place of reason. In spite of my sadness I had sometimes to smile at the violence with which people spoke. Their opinions were basically exaggerations, conceits, fears. But the amusement that comes from watching people make fools of themselves isn't good. There's too much malice in it to please a heart more in key with simple joys. One can feel a mocking gaiety and still remain miserable. I think unhappiness may even engender such feelings. Sour pleasures feed off sour hearts.

The hope brought and so quickly destroyed by the Revolution did not change my mood. I remained out of sorts with my fate, and my discontent was softened only by the kindness and trust of Mme de B. From time to time, during those political arguments whose rancor she tried vainly to reduce, she would glance wistfully at me. Such looks were like balm. They seemed to say that I alone could understand her.

About this time talk started of emancipating the Negroes. Of course this question passionately interested me. I still cherished the illusion that at least somewhere else in the world there were others like myself. I knew they were not happy and I supposed them noble-hearted. I was eager to know what would happen to them. But alas, I soon learned my lesson. The Santo Domingo massacres gave me cause for fresh and heartrending sadness. Till then I had regretted belonging to a race of outcasts. Now I had the shame of belonging to a race of barbarous murderers.

Meanwhile, the Revolution made rapid strides. Alarm spread—the extremists were getting all the posts of power. It soon became clear that they had made up their minds to respect nothing, and after the terrible days in 1792 of June 20th and August 10th anything was possible. What remained of Mme de B.'s circle now dispersed. Some fled persecution by going abroad. Others went into hiding or withdrew to the provinces. Mme de B. did neither, since the closest concern of her heart—a certain memory and its grave—made it impossible for her to leave her home.

We had been living for several months in isolation when, at the end of 1792, the decree announcing the confiscation of the property of those who had escaped abroad was promulgated. Mme de B. would not have worried, in this universal catastrophe, about the loss of her own fortune. But by some family arrangement, she had only a life interest in it—the capital belonged to her grandchildren. She therefore decided to make Charles, the younger of the two brothers, return home. The elder, then aged twenty, was to join the royalist army of Condé outside France. The two young men were at that time in Italy, at the end of the grand tour begun two years earlier in such different circumstances. Charles arrived in Paris at the beginning of February 1793, a little after the execution of the king.

That outrage had caused Mme de B. the most acute grief. She abandoned herself entirely to it, and was courageous enough to feel a horror at the crime proportionate to its enormity. There is something striking about great suffering in the old, since it has the authority of reason. Mme de B. grieved with all the strength of her character. Her health was affected. I did not know how to begin to comfort her, or even distract her. I used to cry, and share her feelings, and tried to raise my soul to hers. The least I could do was to suffer as much as, and with, her.

While the Terror lasted, I seldom thought of my own troubles. I should have been ashamed to feel a victim among so many greater tragedies. In any case all the world was miserable, and I no longer felt alone. A view of life is like a motherland. It is a possession mutually shared. Those who uphold and defend it are like brothers. Sometimes I used to tell myself that, poor negress though I was, I still belonged with all the noblest spirits, because of our shared longing for justice. The day when decency and truth were victorious would be their day of triumph, and mine. But that day was sadly remote.

As soon as Charles was with us again, Mme de B. left Paris for the country. All her friends were now in hiding or in flight. She was reduced to one, an old priest, whom I had heard making fun of religion for the last ten years, but who now grumbled at the selling of church property, which had cost him an income of twenty thousand pounds. He came with us to Saint-Germain. He was a gentle companion, or, rather, easy to get along with. There was nothing truly gentle about his equanimity, which was intellectual rather than spiritual.

All her life Mme de B. had been in a position to render services. As a friend of M. de Choiseul she had been able, during his long ministry, to help many people. Two of the most influential leaders during the Terror had reasons to be grateful to her. They did not renege on their obligations, and never lost her interests from sight. They shielded her—indeed several times risked their own lives to save hers from the fury of the revolutionaries. At that time, as you may know, not even the leaders, in the more extreme parties, could show the smallest kindness without great peril to themselves. It was as if, in this stricken land, evil alone could govern, since it alone got or destroyed authority. Mme de B. was spared prison. She was kept guarded at home, on the pretext of ill health. Charles, the old priest, and myself stayed by her side and cared for her as best we could.

The anxiety and horror of those days are indescribable. Every evening we read of the sentencing and guillotining of friends of Mme de B. We lived in constant dread that her protectors would one day fail to save her from the same fate. We learned later that she had indeed been about to suffer it when Robespierre's death brought this nightmare time to an end. We breathed again. The guards left the house and we four remained in the same solitude and state of mind, I imagine, as those who have together escaped a great disaster. It was as if misfortune had strengthened all the bonds between us. Then, at least, I did not feel myself an outsider.

If after the loss of my childish illusions I've known moments of happiness in my life, they came in the period that followed those grim months. Mme de B. had to the highest degree the qualities that make up the charm of intellect. She was indulgent and open-minded, one could say what one liked in front of her—and she knew how to guess what one really wanted to say behind what one said. She never snubbed people by twisting meanings or by criticizing too harshly. Ideas were taken strictly at face value. One was never called to unreasonable account. If this had been her only virtue, her friends might still have termed themselves fortunate. But she had so many other graces. Her talk was never empty or boring, and everything was food for it. An interest in the trivial can seem futile in ordinary beings. But a person of genius can convert it into the source of a thousand pleasures, because the uniqueness of fine minds is that they can make something out of nothing. The most banal thought became fertile in Mme de B.'s mouth. Her wit and common sense knew how to dress it in a thousand fresh colors.

Charles shared his grandmother's character and intelligence—that is to say, his was what hers must formerly have been . . . shrewd, firm, and open, but without the power of qualification. Youth cannot qualify. For it, everything is either good or bad, whereas the rock upon which old age founders is usually the discovery that nothing is altogether one thing or the other. Charles had the two fine enthusiasms of his age—for justice and for truth. I said before that he hated even the suspicion of affectation, and sometimes he saw it even where it wasn't. It was flattering to be trusted by him. He was reserved by nature, so one knew this trust came not from mere inclination but from personal esteem. All he gave in this way gained value from the fact that he rarely acted without thinking first. Yet nothing about him was forced. He relied greatly on me, telling me every thought he had, and without hesitation. In the evenings, as we sat around a table, our conversations ranged over everything. The old priest would be there. He had manufactured such a complete chain of wrong ideas, and argued for them with such sincerity, that he provided endless fun for Mme de B. Her luminous and unbiased mind knew superbly well how to demonstrate the absurdities of the poor old man's position. He was never angry, though she turned his "categorical ideas" upside down with great shafts of common sense. We used to compare them to the heroic sword blows of Roland and Charlemagne.

Mme de B. was fond of walking and every morning she went on the priest's arm into the forest at Saint-Germain. Charles and I used to follow far behind. It was on these occasions that he used to talk to me of his current preoccupations, of his plans and hopes, of his opinions of the world, of things, men, events. He hid nothing from me, and yet he didn't think of it as a telling of secrets. He had depended on me for so long. To him, my companionship was like existence itself. He enjoyed it without noticing it. I was not required to pay attention, to show interest. He knew very well that when he talked about himself, he talked about me. I was closer to him than he was himself.

The magic of such intimacy is that it can be a substitute for anything—even happiness.

It never occurred to me to talk to Charles of what had made me suffer so much. I used to listen to him and our conversations threw a kind of spell over me. I forgot my troubles. If he had questioned me, I should have remembered them. And then I'd have told him everything. But he never guessed that I too might have secrets. They had all become used to seeing me unwell. Mme de B. tried so hard to make me happy that she must have believed me to be so. I often told myself that I ought to have been. I accused myself of ingratitude, of madness. I don't know if I would ever have dared to admit the extent to which this irremediable stain of my color had made me miserable. There is something humiliating in not knowing how to tolerate the inevitable. And then again, when this kind of misery masters the mind, it has all the appearance of despair.

Another thing that made me shy with Charles was the rather uncompromising turn of his ideas. One evening we were discussing the sentiment of pity and we tried to decide whether the results or the causes of unhappiness inspire the most sympathy. Charles claimed that the causes do. For him all suffering had to have some rational foundation. But who can say what is or isn't rational? Is reason the same for everyone? Do we all feel the same desires? And what is unhappiness if it isn't the lack of what we desire?

But our evening conversations rarely forced me to think of myself. I tried to do so as little as possible. I had removed all the mirrors from my bedroom, I wore gloves all the time, and dresses that hid my neck and arms. When I went out-of-doors I put on a large hat with a veil. I even wore it indoors frequently. In this way I wretchedly deceived myself. Like a child, I shut my eyes, and supposed myself invisible.

Toward the end of 1795, the Terror came to an end. Life began to return to normal. The remnants of Mme de B.'s circle gathered round her again. I saw the number of her friends increase, and with no pleasure at all. My position in the world was so false that the more society got back to its usual ways, the less I felt a part of it. Every time I saw new faces arriving at Mme de B.'s house, I underwent new tortures. The surprise tinged with disapproval that I used to observe in visitors' expressions began to upset me. I knew at once that in a moment I should inevitably be the subject of an aside in one of the window bays, or of some whispered exchange. Naturally the presence of a black woman enjoying the close confidence of Mme de B. had to be explained. These explanations martyred me. I should have liked to be transported back to my uncivilized native land and its savage inhabitants—less frightening to me than this merciless society that declared me guilty of a crime it alone had committed. For days on end I was haunted by its sneering face. I saw it in my dreams, in every waking moment. It stood before me like my own reflection.

Alas, it was really the face of the imaginary monster I had allowed to obsess me. God had not then taught me how to exorcise such delusions. I had still to learn that peace lies in Him alone.

At that time it was in the affection of Charles that I sought sanctuary. I was proud of his friendship, prouder still of his good qualities. For me, he was perfect; I knew nothing better in this world. Before then I'd always believed I loved him as a brother, but since my illness it seemed to me that I'd grown old; and my feelings for him had grown maternal. I think only a mother could have had that passionate desire for his happiness and success in life. I would willingly have given my life to spare him a moment of pain. I realized long before he did himself the effect he had on other people—he was lucky enough not to be bothered by things like that. It was very simple. He had nothing to fear from others, none of my habitual anxiety about what they were thinking of me. In his life everything was harmony. In mine it was discord.

One morning an old friend of Mme de B. called to see her. He came with a marriage proposal for Charles. Mlle de Thémines had become a rich heiress in very distressing circumstances, her entire family having died, and in one day, beneath the guillotine. Her sole surviving relation was a great-aunt, a former nun. She was now the guardian of the young lady and, since she was over eighty years old, saw it as her duty to marry her off as soon as possible. She was frightened of having to leave her niece without family and protection.

Mlle de Thémines had birth, fortune, and upbringing on her side. She was sixteen years old, as pretty as one could wish. A decision was easy. Mme de B. consulted Charles, who at first was rather alarmed at the idea of marrying so young. But soon he felt he would like to see the girl. A meeting took place, and he objected no more.

Anaïs de Thémines might have been invented just to please Charles. She was physically attractive, but without coquettishness. Another charming quality was a modesty so unassuming that one knew she could only have been born with it. Charles was allowed to visit her and soon he fell head over heels in love. He told me how his passion grew, and I was impatient to see this beautiful creature, who was destined to bring so much happiness to him.

At last she came to us at Saint-Germain. Charles had already spoken to her about me and I didn't have to endure that first disdainful scrutiny which always hurt me so deeply. She seemed an angel of kindness, and I assured her she would be happy with Charles. He might seem young, but I knew that even at twenty-one he had the solid sense of a much older man. I answered her many questions about him—she was aware I'd known him since childhood. Nothing gave me greater pleasure than to praise him, and I talked on and on.

The celebration of the marriage was delayed for some weeks while the details of the contract were settled. Charles continued to visit his bride-to-be and often he stayed in Paris for two or three days at a time. I suffered from these absences and blamed myself for putting my own happiness above Charles's. That had never previously been a prerequisite of my regard for him. The days when he did return were like holidays to me. He would tell me of all that had happened; and if he had seen a growing return of his love in Anaïs, I was happy for him and with him. However, one day he talked about how he wished their marriage to be.

"I want to have her entire trust, I want her to have mine. I shan't hide anything, she shall know my every thought, every secret feeling of my heart. I want a trust between us exactly like yours and mine."

"*Exactly like yours and mine!*" That phrase cut deep. It reminded me that Charles ignored the solitary secret of my life. At the same time it took away my longing to tell him of it.

Gradually Charles's absences became almost continuous. He was never more than brief moments at Saint-

Germain, coming on horseback to save time on the journey. After dinner he returned to the city. Thus he was never there in the evenings. Mme de B. made little jokes about his new fidelity to Paris. If only I could have done the same!

We were one day in the forest. Charles had been away nearly all the week, but now I suddenly saw him at the end of the clearing through the forest down which we were walking. He galloped up and dismounted, and then began to stroll with us. After a few minutes of general conversation, he fell behind with me and we began to talk in the old way. I remarked on it.

"In the old way?" he said with some surprise. "But how different it was, Ourika. Did I ever really have anything to say then? I feel as if I've only started to live these last two months. I can't tell you what I feel for Anaïs. Sometimes it's as if my whole being enters hers—looks she gives me, they stop my breath. If anything makes her blush, I want to fall at her feet and adore her. When I think how divinely innocent she is, that she's to be in my care, that she's giving me her life, her future . . . it makes me delirious with happiness. I want to be everything that makes her happy. The father and mother she lost. But I'll be her husband too, her lover. I'm the very first man she's ever been in love with, she'll pour her feelings into mine, we shall be one life. And when it's all over, I want her to be able to say that I never gave her a single hour's unhappiness. Can you imagine what it's like? To realize that she'll be the mother of my children, that they will take life from her? They'll be just like her, so gentle. Beautiful. Dear God, what have I done to deserve such luck?"

By then I was sadly asking God a very different question. Long before the end of this fervent confession I'd felt something I can't describe. God will bear witness, I was happy for Charles. But why had that same God given poor Ourika life? Why wasn't it ended on that slaver from which she had been snatched—or at her mother's breast? A handful of African sand would have been enough to cover my small body, and I should have found it a light burden. What did the world care whether I lived? Why was I condemned to exist? Unless it was to live alone, always alone, and never loved. I prayed God not to let it be like this, to remove me from the face of the earth. Nobody needed me, I was isolated from all.

This terrible thought gripped me with more violence than ever before. I felt myself sway, I fell to my knees, my eyes closed, and I thought I was going to die there and then.

*As she said those last words, the melancholy of the poor nun seemed to increase. Her voice faded away and some tears began to seep down her wasted cheeks. I wanted her to interrupt her story. But she refused.*

"It's nothing," she said. "The agony isn't in my heart any more. The root has been cut off. God has taken pity on me. He led me back from the abyss. I threw myself into it only because I didn't understand it—fell in love with it. You mustn't forget that I'm happy now." She sighed. "Though that was the last thing I was in those days."

Until the time I've just mentioned, I bore my suffering. It had affected my health, but I'd kept sane—some sort of control over myself. My misery, like a maggot in a fruit, had begun with the core. In my heart I carried a seed of death, even when outwardly I seemed full of life. I still enjoyed conversation, argument made me lively. I had even retained a kind of artificial sense of humor. But I'd lost all touch with real happiness. In a word, until then I'd been stronger than my troubles. But now they had become too strong for me.

Charles carried me back to the house. The usual remedies were tried, and I regained consciousness. As I opened my eyes again, I saw Mme de B. beside my bed. Charles held my hand. They had been my doctors and I saw in their faces a mixture of anxiety and self-reproach. It touched me very deeply. I felt life flow back through me, and I burst into tears. Mme de B. gently wiped them away. She said nothing and asked no questions, while Charles overwhelmed me with them. I can't remember how I replied, I made up something about the heat, the length of the walk. He accepted this explanation and I felt resentful again when he did. My tears ended. I told myself how very easy it was to deceive those whose interests lay elsewhere. He was still holding my hand. I took it away and tried to seem composed.

Charles left as usual at five o'clock, and I was also hurt by that. I wanted him to be worried—I was in such agony. He would still have left; I would have forced him to go. But then I'd have been able to think that he owed me his happiness in Paris that evening. The idea would have consoled me. I took very good care not to show this secret wish to Charles. Unspoken desires have a kind of modesty—if they are not guessed, they can't be satisfied. It's as if they need two people to exist.

Charles had hardly ridden away when I began to run a high temperature. The following two days, it grew worse. Mme de B. looked after me with all her usual kindness of heart: in despair at the state of my health and at how she should now get me to Paris, where Charles's marriage was to take place on the morrow. The doctors told her that my life would not be in danger if she left me at Saint-Germain. She accepted their decision, though she was so tenderly affectionate to me before she left that for a brief time I was calmer.

However, very soon after her departure the literal and total isolation in which I now found myself for the first time in my life threw me into a state of profound hopelessness. I saw the possibility I had so often imagined become certainty. I was dying, cut off from everyone I loved. They couldn't even hear the sobbing that would have troubled their joy. I saw them drowned in their own intense happiness, remote from me as I lay on my deathbed. In my life I had only them; but they had no need of me. Nobody had need of me. This appalling awareness of the futility of one's existence is the most damaging of all emotions. It gave me such a loathing of life that I sincerely wanted to die of the illness that had attacked me.

I didn't speak, I gave virtually no sign of consciousness. I could think only one thing: *I want to die.* There were brief periods when I was less calm. I remembered each word of that last conversation with Charles in the forest. I saw him floating through that sea of delight he had described, while I died abandoned, as solitary in death as in life. This idea obsessed me even more painfully than my unhappiness. I gave myself daydreams to assuage it, I pictured Charles returning from his marriage to Saint-Germain. The servants would say: *She has died.* And would you believe it, I savored his imagined grief with joy. It was my revenge. But on whom was it my revenge? On someone who all my life had given me nothing but affection and encouragement.

I soon saw the horror of these frightful imaginings and dimly realized that even though unhappiness may not be a sin, to abandon oneself to it as I had done was without excuse. My ideas took another course. I tried to conquer myself, to find some strength inside me to combat these feelings that tore me apart. But I didn't look for this strength where it truly resides. I blamed myself for my ingratitude. I told myself I would die, I wished to die; but I would never let this passionate envy enter my heart. I was a disinherited child, but I still had my innocence. I would not let that be withered by lack of charity. I was to pass through this world like a shadow; but in the grave I would find peace.

By now the newly married couple would already be in paradise. So let them have Ourika's happiness also, let her fall as the leaf falls in autumn. Had I not suffered enough?

I recovered from the illness that had put my life in danger, but only to lapse into a state of listlessness largely founded on my affliction. Mme de B. made her home at Saint-Germain after Charles's marriage. He came often there with Anaïs—never without her. I always suffered far worse when they were with us. I don't know whether it was the picture of happiness they presented that made my own evil fate harder to bear, or whether it was the proximity of Charles, with all its reminders of our former closeness. I tried sometimes to discover his old self, but I no longer knew him. It wasn't that he didn't still talk almost as freely to me as in the past; but his present attitude was no more like the old than an artificial flower is like a real one. They may look alike. But only one has a fragrance, and life.

Charles attributed the change in my character to the deterioration of my health. I suspect that Mme de B. was a better judge of the true state of my mind, that she guessed what secretly racked my being—and I suspect that it upset her deeply. But it was long past the time when I could reassure other people. All my pity was for myself.

Anaïs became pregnant and we returned to Paris. The pain of my life increased every day. A tranquil domestic happiness, the gentle bonds of family, a marriage still at its stage of innocence, always so tender, so passionate—it was no sight for a victim of fate destined to pass her wretched life in solitude. Destined to die without having once been loved. Without having known any other human relationships than those of dependence and charity.

Days, months passed like this. I took no part in conversation, I had given up all my painting and singing. If I still managed to read a little, it was in books where I saw some kind of portrayal—though it was never bleak enough—of the despair that consumed me. I concocted a new poison, I used to get drunk on my own tears. Alone in my bedroom for hours on end, I abandoned myself to pain.

The birth of a son came as a climax to Charles's happiness. He ran to tell me the good news and I recognized in his excitement and joy traces of our old intimacy. It hurt most terribly, that voice of a friend I no longer had. Memory ripped the wound open again.

Charles's son was as pretty as the mother. The sight of Anaïs with her baby ravished everyone. I alone was obliged, by a perverse fate, to view them sourly. I glutted myself emotionally on this vision of a happiness I could never know. Envy circled in my heart like a vulture. What harm had I ever done those who had pretended to save me by bringing me to this land of exile? Why hadn't I been left to follow my own destiny?

What did it matter that I might now have been the black slave of some rich planter? Scorched by the sun, I should be laboring on someone else's land. But I would have a poor hut of my own to go to at day's end; a partner in my life, children of my own race who would call me their mother, who would kiss my face without disgust, who would rest their heads against my neck and sleep in my arms. I had done nothing—and yet here I was, condemned never to know the only feelings my heart was created for.

I prayed God to take me from this world. I could no longer endure living in it.

Kneeling in my bedroom, I was still making this suicidal request when I heard the door open. It was Mme de B.'s friend, the marquise. She had only recently returned from England, where she had spent several years during

39

the Revolution. When I saw her approach, I felt something like panic, since the sight of her always reminded me that it had been she who first opened my eyes to my real situation. She had introduced me into that mine of sorrow I had so deeply exploited. Since her return to Paris, I could never see her without a feeling of distress.

"I've come to have a little chat with you, my dear Ourika. You know I've always been fond of you, ever since you were a child. And it makes me very sad indeed to see what a low state you've got yourself into. Don't you think a girl of your intelligence ought to find a brighter side to things?"

"Madame, intelligence only makes real misfortunes seem worse. It makes them take so many different forms."

"But if the misfortunes can't be remedied? Isn't it a madness to refuse to accept their existence? To fight as you do against the inevitable? After all, this isn't a battle anyone can ever win."

"I know. But then it follows that the inevitability is just one more misfortune."

"But in that case you'd agree, Ourika, that common sense suggests resignation and distraction."

"Yes. But distraction is impossible where there is no hope."

"You could at least find things you like doing—things to help you pass your time."

"Madame, forced interests are forced. They hold no pleasure."

"Come now. You have many gifts."

"Such gifts can help only when you have a purpose in life. But mine would be like the flower of that English poet—'born to blush unseen and waste its sweetness on the desert air.'"[1]

"Aren't you forgetting the pleasure you might give your friends?"

"I have no friends, Madame. I have protectors. And that's not the same thing at all."

"Ourika, you're making yourself very miserable. And all to no purpose."

"Nothing has purpose in my life. Not even my unhappiness."

"But how dare you judge yourself so harshly! You of all people, who stayed alone and so devotedly at your mistress's side during the Terror?"

I murmured sadly, "I'm like those evil spirits who have power only in times of calamity. They disappear when times are good."

"Tell me your secret, my poor Ourika. Open your heart. Nobody is more concerned for you than I am. And perhaps I can help you."

---

[1]Thomas Gray, "Elegy Written in a Country Churchyard" (1751)

41

"I have no secret, Madame. You know very well what my problems are. My social situation. And the color of my skin."

"Nonsense. You can't deny that locked away inside you is some deep trouble. One can see it at a glance."

I persisted in repeating what I had already said. She became angry, her voice rose. And I knew the storm was about to break.

"Is this your open nature? The honesty everyone admires in you? I warn you, Ourika. Reserve can sometimes lead to lies."

"Very well! And what could I tell you, madame—you of all people? You predicted long ago the hell I now know. I have nothing to add to your prophecy. Especially to you."

"That is one thing you will never convince me of," she said. "But since you refuse me your trust, since you pretend there's no secret at the bottom of all this, very fine—I shall take it on myself to inform you that there is. Yes, my child. All your misery, all your suffering comes from just one thing: an insane and doomed passion for Charles. And if you weren't madly in love with him, you could come perfectly well to terms with being black. I wish you good day, Ourika. I'm going now. And make no mistake, with far less sympathy for you than when I entered this room."

She left my room as soon as she had spoken those last words. I stood there as if struck by lightning. What she had just revealed to me threw a terrifying illumination

42

over the depths of my suffering. It was like the shaft of
light that once penetrated to the bottom of hell and made
the miserable beings there weep for the darkness of their
existence. Had what had cancered my heart really been
no more than a forbidden love? That longing to have a
place in the chain of being, that need of natural affection,
that agonized fear of isolation—no more than the sour
by-products of a forbidden lust? When I thought I was
merely envying the idea of being happily married, was my
own imagined happiness with the husband the real spur
of my wicked dreams?

I couldn't see what it was in my actions that could have
led anyone to believe me infected by a doomed love for
Charles. Was it impossible to love anything beyond one's
own existence innocently? A mother who risked death to
save a son—what drove her to such a sacrifice? All those
brothers and sisters who chose to die together on the scaf-
fold, and who prayed together before they mounted the
steps—was the love that united them a guilty one? Did a
day pass in the world when some humanitarian instinct
did not produce an act of sublime self-sacrifice? Why then
could I not love Charles, the childhood friend, my champion in adolescence, in the same way?

But all through this, a mysterious voice cried deep
in my heart: she is right, I am guilty. I called to God in
outrage. Had my ravaged heart now to find room for
remorse? Had I to taste every bitterness, exhaust every

form of pain? Even my tears now would be illegitimate. It would be forbidden even to think of him. Even to suffer must be a sin.

These terrible thoughts threw me into a state of collapse not unlike death. That same night, I ran a high fever. Not three days later, my life was feared for. The doctor declared that if I was to receive the last sacraments, there was not a moment to be lost. A servant was sent for my confessor, only to learn that he had just died. Mme de B. summoned a parish priest. He came and administered extreme unction, for I was by then too ill for the viaticum. I had lost consciousness and my death was expected at any moment.

No doubt it was at this point that God took pity on me. He began by preserving my life. Against all expectation, my remnant of strength stayed firm. I fought for two weeks, then consciousness returned. Mme de B. never left my side, and Charles seemed to have rediscovered his old affection for me. The priest continued to visit me each day, since he wanted to hear my confession as soon as I was in a fit state. I wished to make it myself. Some instinct drove me toward God. I felt the need to throw myself into His arms and find peace there.

The priest heard the confession of my sins. He showed no shock at the state of my soul. Like an old sailor, he had experience of such hurricanes. He began by reassuring me on this love of which I was accused.

44

"Your heart is innocent," he said. "You have hurt only yourself. But for all that, you are guilty. God will one day ask you to account for the possibility of happiness He bestowed on you. And what have you done with it? This happiness was in your own hands, since our happiness lies in doing our duty. I wonder if you have ever known your duty, let alone performed it. God is the purpose of man. Yet what has your purpose been? But you must take heart, my child, and pray to Him. He waits with open arms. For Him there is neither black nor white. All hearts are equal in His eyes. And yours promises to be worthy."

Thus this good man encouraged me. His simple words brought a hitherto unknown peace into my soul. I reflected endlessly on them and, as if from some rich subterranean gallery, kept finding new matter for thought. I realized that I had indeed never recognized my proper responsibilities. God has ordained them to the solitary as much as to those in society. If He has deprived some people of family, He has given them all mankind as a substitute. A nun, I told myself, may have renounced everything, but she is not alone in the world. She has chosen a family, she is a mother to the orphan, a daughter to the aged, a sister to all misfortune. Haven't normally sociable men often chosen a voluntary retreat? They need to be alone with God, they want to give up all pleasure in order to worship in solitude the pure source of all good and all peace of mind; to work, in their innermost hearts, to

45

make their souls worthy to stand before the Creator. It is to please Him that we delight in refining our spiritual lives, in adorning them, as if for some celebration, with all the virtues that He values highest.

How had I behaved, alas? The unreasoning toy of instinct, I had chased after the pleasures of life and neglected true happiness. But it is still not too late. Perhaps God, in casting me into this alien land, wished to bring me to Him without my knowing. He rescued me from savagery and ignorance. By a miracle of charity He stole me from the evils of slavery and taught me His law. It shows me what I must do, my road—and I shall follow it now. Never again shall I use His gifts to offend Him. Never again shall He be accused of my weaknesses.

This new light on my situation brought calm back to my mind. I was astonished at the peace that followed so many storms. An outlet had been opened to the flood torrent that destroyed its own banks. Now at last its pacified waves fell into a tranquil sea.

I decided to become a nun. I told Mme de B., who took the announcement sadly. But finally she agreed.

"I've done you so much harm in wishing to do you good. I don't feel I have the right to oppose you now."

Charles resisted the idea more strongly. He begged me, beseeched me to stay with his mother.

I said to him, "Let me go, Charles, to the one place where I may still think of you day and night . . ."

*Here the young nun abruptly ended her story. I continued to attend her, but my science proved sadly unavailing. She died at the end of October, with the last of the autumn leaves.*